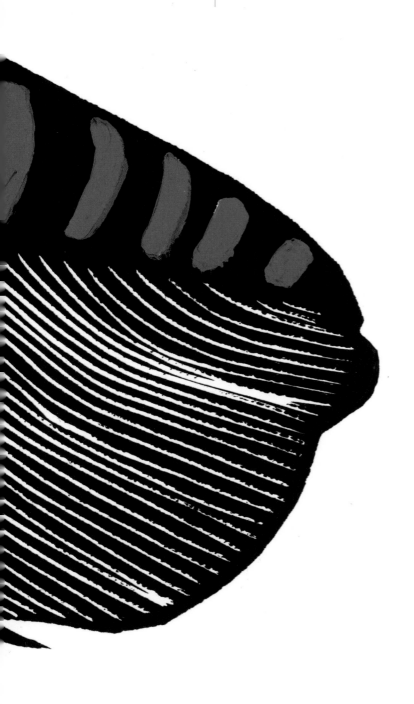

This Will Last Forever

Pushkin Press
Somerset House, Strand
London WC1R 1LA1

Original title: Dit gaat nooit voorbij © text & illustrations Octavie Wolters,
Uitgeverij Ploegsma / Amsterdam 2024

English language translation © Michele Hutchison 2025

First published by Pushkin Press in 2025

The publisher gratefully acknowledges the support of
the Dutch Foundaton for Literature

N ederlands
letterenfonds
dutch foundation
for literature

1 3 5 7 9 8 6 4 2

ISBN 13: 978-1-78269-529-5

Typeset by Felicity Awdry

Printed and bound in China by C&C Offset Printing Co., Ltd.

www.pushkinpress.com

THIS WILL LAST FOREVER
by Octavie Wolters

Translated by Michele Hutchison

January

At home I have a basket full of the short lengths of wool I've kept over the years. They've ended up in a big knot. I never do any knitting, I can't stand it, but occasionally I need a particular colour to repair something. I'll try to get the right thread out of the basket, but if I pull too hard the whole tangle only gets worse.

I'm reminded of this as I go for a walk in the forest. It is New Year's Day, the water in the mere is a dark indigo, the sky grey. The poplars are lined up, stark and bare. Nature is never uncluttered, but in winter it makes a brave attempt.

A blackbird is sitting on a branch.

'Aren't you cold?' I ask it.

'Cold?' asks the blackbird.

He ruffles his feathers. It sounds like he's never thought about it before. I feel a little bit sorry for him, such a small bird in such a big, dark forest. I want to tell him things will get better, it will get warmer. I think of everything hidden in the wet earth under the trees, of everything yet to come.

'The snowdrops will pop up again soon, and then spring will come, bringing poppies and mayweed.'

I hold my hands out towards the barren fields and the marshland on the other side of the path as if to show them to him.

'Everything will turn green again.'

'Really?' says the blackbird.

I'm not sure he cares very much.

Of course, I reflect, the coming spring doesn't exist to a blackbird. The future brimming with corn and a pond full of frogs doesn't exist. Neither does last summer, nor January, nor the first day of a new year.

All a blackbird knows is what he sees. Everything hidden is also hidden in his mind.

It makes me a little jealous, though I'm not quite sure why.

A blackbird knows the indigo mere, the bare trees, he knows what the branch he sits on feels like beneath his feet.

Dusk falls, the sky slowly brightens, behind the poplars the moon appears.

The blackbird flies from his branch and disappears from sight.

I imagine him flying at the same speed as the passing time, just as slow and just as fast.

February

It froze last night. I'm wearing my new padded leather boots, and I'm still a bit doubtful I'll ever become friends with these stiff clumpy fellows. I had to throw away my previous pair, a tragedy. I'd had them for at least a decade, and they were exactly the way I liked them: bare-nosed but forgiving and obedient. They never complained and were always up for a good walk. But their soles were cracked through, so I sulkily had to order myself some new ones.

First I hear the wren, a rustling of leaves, and only then do I see it, pecking around beneath the snowdrops.

'Funny, it was still bare there yesterday,' I say.

The embankment at the edge of the woods seems to have been carpeted over-night with little white bells. They are growing over the protruding tree roots, sheltered by the undergrowth. As far as I was concerned, it was barren and muddy all winter, until today.

'Bare? Do you think so?' the wren asks.

He's looking for something to eat.

I can't get over the fact that for the past few weeks bulbs have been growing under the ground, sprouting stalks and leaves, without me being aware of them.

'Even if I sat and watched a plant all day, I'd never really see it grow,' I tell the wren.

He flies onto the lower branch of a cherry tree and looks at me.

'Maybe some things just happen,' he says, 'We don't have to see everything.'

I realise that I'm not entirely satisfied with this answer. When something isn't visible but does exist, you enter an ambiguous zone where everything is just guesswork.

Feeling grumpy, I step onto one of the frozen puddles on the path. Between the water and the ice, there's a layer of nothing. This is cat ice, the space left after some water under the ice drains away. The ice cracks, my winter boots sink into the mud. At least they are waterproof, one nil to them.

'There are some things you just have to accept,' the wren says.

I shrug.

I find it a complicated idea, I prefer my secrets unravelled. A nothingness, an empty space feels so inadequate sometimes.

'I'll do my best,' I say.

'Good,' says the wren.

March

The time has come. It has been below zero for six days in a row. I throw my skates over the barbed wire fence around the field and crawl under it. The snow is brittle and powdery after all the frost, the slope shines white between the trees. A fox's footprints run along the path. The cows are out. They don't seem to be cold, but they are curious. The group of seven yearlings crowd around me as I pull off my snow boots at the edge of the mere and lace up my skates. As they snuffle my neck, their warmth feels like something from the past.

The ice on the shallow lake is as transparent as glass. I see the water plants silent in the darkness below me, bubbles like exhaled breath.

'I'm so scared sometimes,' I say to the lapwing.

Lapwings don't like frost; he won't have been expecting this cold.

'What of?' he asks.

I feel the thin iron of my skates tap the ice, miraculous really, only a razor-sharp slash holds me to the world today.

'Of everything,' I reply.

The ice sings, the sound carries across the frozen lake, for a moment I can almost see it, then it dies away in the bushes on the bankside.

I'm afraid of everything outside, of nasty things, accidents, disasters, loss, heights, depths, noise, people. But most of all I am afraid inside. A fear that shifts along with my breathing, black and billowing. I cannot see it, I can only feel it, like a memory whose image just won't sharpen.

'I can talk to the fears outside,' I tell the lapwing.

'I can tell them to shut up, be quiet. I can silence them for a while when I've had enough.

But the fear inside is woven into me.'

I look out over the snowy landscape.

I think the fear belongs to me now. It has become a part of me, an essential organ.

'I worry I'll cease to exist without it.'

The lapwing flies up and settles again, the reeds vibrating so loudly I can't even hear my own thoughts.

'Maybe you can't exist without it,' he says.

Fear, an eternal companion I cannot shake off.

For a second, the thought is even more suffocating than usual.

Then I'm overwhelmed by a wondrous sense of peace.

April

The sun is shining and the air suddenly feels warmer today, though it is a somewhat self-satisfied warmth with an undertone of chilly draughts. The earth is still breathing out the frost that soaked into it over the long winter, which hasn't simply come to an end, of course.

It doesn't bother the dog, who bounds into the bog with paws sloshing, before coming out pitch black. I think of the amount of mud she has taken with her throughout the years, it must amount to kilos and kilos of it. And all into my house.

'I have long thought that comfort is a futile thing,' I say to the great tits.

They chatter away in the blossom above my head.

The fields are brown, just a green haze here and there. The light is glaring, the sky transparent. I can see all the way to the end.

'Why?' they ask.

I look out over the pasture, which is empty too, the cows have just been brought in for milking. The farmer is a sturdy man, big moustache, overalls. I'm always touched by the way the cows let him pet them like puppies. His old manor farm is not far from here, a beautiful set of buildings dating back to the fifteenth century. There's even a little chapel.

I reflect for a while.

'Comfort has always seemed so small to me, so fragile.'

I search for words. 'Comfort made me feel so powerless.'

I don't know if I've explained it properly and hold my tongue for a while as the birds fly back and forth with bits of moss for their nests.

I have long clung onto hope, to expectation, in one form or another. I have clung to the idea that everything is good for something. As long as I could find reasons for things, I was in control.

A few marsh marigolds are in bloom, and bright green milkweed. I would love to pluck some of the cow parsley already cautiously growing here and there along the ditch, but ever since someone told me that picking it brings bad luck I don't dare.

You never know.

I think of the past few years. Disease and death slunk around, life rumbled and shook in its foundations. All hope drifted away, leaving me lonely and disillusioned. There was nothing left to hold onto.

The great tits have fallen silent. They are resting on a gnarled old branch.

'Comfort means surrender,' I say.

The great tits nod, their little black beaks gleaming in the spring light, their feathers ruffled. I am moved by how dishevelled they look. Two soft warm little balls.

'Comfort is there when everything else has long gone,' they say.

May

Last night I dreamt about the time, long ago, when my dog was a puppy. She lay in my lap, a big lump, her chubby body seeking my warmth. I bent over her, covered her with my hands. She was so soft. I woke up feeling tender.

Now the big lump is standing on the bank of the stream, her fur tangled from the wet grass, muzzle covered in dirt, contemplating whether to jump into the brown soup.

I'm reminded of a few years ago when there was a dead deer in the stream. I only saw it when the water level dropped during the spring and its skeleton was slowly revealed, bit by bit. A skull, a ribcage, the hind legs, the sinking water slowly uncovering everything, like a mystery that had taken place in the dead of winter.

There's no dead deer today, spring is light and simple, with low-flying swallows. Sometimes they come so close I can practically feel their wings brush my face. The weather is warm but overcast, I've put on my mackintosh just in case. The clammy air makes its sleeves stick to my bare arms.

It is an unexpectedly pleasant feeling.

'Sometimes something happens without anyone in the world knowing about it,' I say.

It's a crazy thought, for a moment I wonder if things actually happen when no one is there to witness them.

Three swallows skim over my head and I try to imagine what happened to the deer. She was attacked, or became sick, weakened by hunger. She fell into the water and didn't have the strength to hoist herself up.

Maybe.

'Sometimes all we can do is make up a story,' I say. 'That's all.'

The swallows nod in agreement.

The tufted vetch is already climbing high up in the meadow, clinging to the barbed wire fence, countless little ladders with purple clusters of flowers between them. Beautiful, I think.

The thought of the deer makes me feel a little melancholic, as if coming up with a story doesn't do it enough justice. After all, she's dead, that's no small thing. Or yes, maybe it is.

I watch the swallows fly over the cornfield that looks like a heaving sea.

All I can do is imagine how it was, how it went, how it felt.

Especially that: how it felt.

June

Every year when I walk along the path beside the stream on warm June days I'm reminded of a wedding. The young bride is nature, and her veil is made of cow parsley. It grows in wide swathes along the bank. It is voile and lace, and it smells like honey.

I think back to my own wedding. I didn't wear a veil, a simple white dress was enough, love I had in abundance. In my hair, I had tucked gypsophila, 'Baby's Breath', which seemed appropriate in a way.

'It's odd how there are so many sounds, yet it seems quiet here,' I say to the little blackcap.

He has perched beside me, clinging to a long stem in a clump of foxgloves growing in the shade of the trees.

We listen to the lapwings, the cry of a buzzard, a flock of greenfinches, the ears of corn rattling. I think it's one of the most beautiful sounds, a cornfield rattling. You have to know about it, otherwise you won't hear it.

'A few years ago, I kept bees,' I tell the blackcap. 'Sometimes I'd rest my head on the hive to hear them buzzing. It's unbelievable, the sound a hive makes. Quite unique, unlike anything I'd ever heard before.'

My father had given me a hive of bees for my birthday. He'd been a beekeeper since my earliest childhood, his hives were at the bottom of our garden. I grew up with bees buzzing around me. I used to let them crawl over my hands as I studied their soft bodies.

You don't buy bees, you have to be given them, so I was overjoyed with my own. We hung the combs in the frames together. I felt part of the swarm, part of the colony. There was a special kind of connection between thousands of little lives and me, the human who cared for them.

The blackcap looks at me.

'Maybe the sounds have been there forever,' he suggests.

I nod.

'We carry them inside us.'

I think of my ancestors, centuries ago. They knew the mew of the buzzard, the lengthy cries of the lapwings, the thousands of young frogs in the water in spring-time. The buzzing of a colony of bees. They stored the sounds in their bodies or minds, they carried them with them, and to me, and now I am here, and they are inside me.

'It's not silence but an echo,' I reflect.

The sounds of all the animals around me, of the fields and the wind, of the gurgling water in the stream, the young leaves on the poplars find their echo in me. I catch them and sense all those who have gone before me.

It is not silence but a deep kind of recognition.

July

A cloud of dust hangs over the path the horses just took. I pluck a few twigs from my hair and brush down my clothes. I like horses when they are safe behind a fence, I find them rather large when they are not. For everyone's sake, I had retreated into the bushes along the path for a moment.

'Are you alright?' the rider had asked, high in their saddle, laughing at me hiding. I'd muttered something unintelligible back.

Meadowsweet and hollyhock grow along the stream. The water is a bright blue, I can see the warm air vibrating above the meadow. I can smell chicory and chamomile. I can't handle the heat that has been lingering for weeks, the dryness of the land tugging at my veins, and yet at the same time my chest bursts with happiness at the sight of the countryside in full bloom, at the apex of the year. It evokes an immense sense of freedom.

It's a strange contradiction.

'If I'm perfectly honest,' I tell the black-headed gulls, 'I don't like forests much.'

I don't often spot black-headed gulls around here. I see them at the lakes near the river's estuary where we often sail our boat. It's only a simple wooden sailing boat, nothing fancy. We love it because it allows us to get close to the banks, our heads barely above the water level. The islands are off-limits to humans, and I love nothing better than anchoring in a small inlet on a languid summer's day and watching the waterbirds preening for hours.

'I'm a woman of the horizon, of open fields, meadows. Forests are too cramped for me. If I can't see into the distance, I feel confined.'

The black-headed gulls fly high above me and dive down to the blue water. My hand sheltering my eyes, I watch them land and immediately take off again.

'Is that so?' they call out, their voices hoarse.

I look around, imagining what the gulls can see from high above me in the sky. Funny I'm only noticing it now. I may be in the middle of open fields, but every side is bordered by dense trees that stretch for miles inland.

Of course, the horizon is never infinite.

I look at my feet, the dusty path under my sandals.

The billions of tiny stones that make up the sand and dirt.

Maybe freedom has nothing to do with the environment at all, nothing to do with woods, open fields, water. The only boundaries are inside yourself.

August

Not so far away, a beech tree fell down last winter, right across the narrow river. A group of children are climbing the wide trunk, filthy bare feet on the slippery bark before jumping, screaming into the water. It's just at the bend, which is convenient, it's deep enough there, they won't get hurt.

I watch for a while, it's lovely. As a child I used to jump into any water I came across in the summer. Wearing just my knickers because they'd dry quickly enough.

I walk on through the fields. The sound of the children's voices dies away, the horizon shimmers.

'The world inside me is as big as the world outside,' I say to the sparrow.

He looks up for a moment from the tansy at the edge of the mere. Even though he is just a small, light bird, I'm still amazed that the slender stem can hold him.

'You can't see it though,' he replies.

It's a clear day, the cattails are blooming in the marsh, purple-pink tufts everywhere between the gullies of water.

'Well, you can't see it,' I say. 'You have to imagine it.'

I look out over the water for a while, young fish darting back and forth in the warm shallows.

'Then what does it look like inside you?' the sparrow asks.

I have to think about that.

It's crazy, although I can picture everything, the words seem to dissolve even before they reach my mouth. I know so many words, but they rarely fit my thoughts.

I think of all the paths and roads in my head, the memories, future dreams, everything in the here and now, what I am working on or doing. But the words stagnate and I remain silent.

Something rustles in the tall grass of the nearby meadow. A fawn? I scan the surroundings hopefully, in search of a young deer's floppy ears.

All I can see is the smooth surface of the water in which clouds drift by. I lean forward slightly and now I can see the reflection of the sparrow and myself too.

'That's it,' I say suddenly. 'This is what I mean.'

I point at our reflections.

'That is what it feels like. My world inside is a mirror of the world outside. And vice versa.'

It is a world of images, words are unnecessary.

The sparrow is also watching us together in the blue water.

The fish flash by us as if they are our thoughts.

'I see,' says the sparrow.

September

I love September. The edges of the days slowly soften, the light dims, the noise hushes. I love the cooler evenings, rainy sometimes, when the fair-weather walkers stay away and the great outdoors becomes mine again.

I've been thinking a lot about loss these past few days, and what it entails exactly. I lost my first baby before we'd even met. I buried a small wooden box in the cold ground, and I remember the way my arms shrank with emptiness afterwards. A longing to hold something, so fierce and painful it was almost concrete.

I pause by the long straight stream that runs between the field on the one side and the meadow on the other. For a few days now I have been seeing a lot of new beaver tracks. Next to me, a great tit has landed on the browning blackberry bushes.

'Something can be there and not there at the same time,' I say.

The tit gives me a questioning look.

I hear something in the water before I see it. Two nostrils, a wet head, two plodding forelegs. The beaver looks at me for a moment before diving. He disappears into one of the burrows in the bank, as if there were another world down there. I wonder how many different worlds there are.

The wind picks up, the tall grass is damp. It is gradually getting too cold for my sandals.

I think of the tiny baby who, so heart-breakingly, was no longer there, but became a new kind of presence. Something I could not ignore.

I hadn't known such a thing existed.

'How did you deal with the loss?' the great tit asks.

I realise a tear is rolling down my cheek.

'I waited,' I say.

I waited until a space revealed itself that was exactly the size of my grief. It was a big space, but I also turned out to have much more space inside than I had ever imagined. That's where I put all my love. I cradled it and nurtured it.

The great tit hops a little closer.

'Has it gone away now?'

'No,' I say.

Loss never goes away.

But the pain of emptiness can be filled.

My baby is inside me, I have given it a body of love.

October

It is still early, I got up in the small hours to see the dew. The field looks woolly in the low sun, the edge of the forest still dark, the hill soft and undulating. While winter can seem to have been arranged in neat right angles, everything now is still breathing the round, plump contours of summer.

I've taken off my anklet. I don't wear jewellery, but during the summer months, I put on a silver chain around my ankle. It's so fine it's barely visible. But this morning I took it off, pulled on a pair of socks and got out my winter boots again that leave a trail through the white grass. I've finally got used to them.

I like to think dew exists to get us used to the idea of the coming frost. The leaves already seem to have a layer of hoarfrost as if to say: the cold is on its way, folks. Won't be long now!

'Sometimes I'd like to unzip myself,' I say to the magpie.

He sits high in the tree and looks down at me, the little human on the ground.

Magpies are so beautiful, I love their black-and-white plumage, their smooth bodies, their long tails that flip up so beautifully when they have just landed.

'And then what?' he asks.

'I'd take a look inside myself.'

The sky is golden, if I tilt my head I can see the silver lining around every cloud, a glow around every branch. There's a layer of fallen leaves under the poplars. I can smell tannic acid, it is one of my favourite smells. It calms me, the quiet time is coming.

'And then what?'

'Then I would check if everything were still alright. Whether my heart hadn't secretly broken for example.'

The magpie lifts his beak in the air as if pondering this for a moment.

'And if your heart had secretly broken, what would you do?'

'I would hold it,' I say, 'until it got better again.'

We stand there for a while, the magpie in the tree and me. The sun is creeping towards its highest point for the day, the dew has evaporated, the gold has migrated to the forest edge. In the meadow, only the snapdragon and vetch are still blooming, and some yarrow here and there.

'It's a good idea, holding a heart,' he says.

He understands.

Then he flies off, circles the tree and squawks out to me goodbye.

November

Two hikers are sitting on a tree trunk next to the path. There are no benches; it's not a recreational nature reserve, thankfully. They aren't locals judging by their clothes: zip-off trousers, hiking boots from an expensive brand, a backpack. I wonder how they ended up here. I consider telling them that immediately behind them there's a meandering stream. You can't see it from here because it's at least ten feet down and well hidden. In the summer, it's lovely under the tall trees, the bubbling water far below.

I nod in greeting but get no response.

That makes the decision easier.

No stream for them.

At the mere, I find three oystercatchers, who are a lot friendlier. They scurry along the water's edge and greet me happily with their long beaks. Together we look out over the marsh, the empty poplars, the fields.

'I've taken a lot of footsteps here,' I say, 'I must have worn the path down by a few inches at least.'

'Haha,' the oystercatchers laugh. 'Hahaha.'

I'm no globetrotter. I enjoy my immediate surroundings, small and contained. I know my country well, and yet it shows me something new every day. I don't have to go far, this is where I find my answers. And my questions. They are just as important.

I like the thought that I have walked the landscape, that I have brought something to it, that I have made a change, however small.

'I never know the purpose of anything, of humans, of the world, or life,' I say to the oystercatchers. 'Or of me'

'You don't need to know that, do you?' they reply.

I nod. I think they are right.

It's alright the way it is.

Everything is there, that's reason enough.

I say goodbye to them and walk back the same way, which I rarely do. I usually walk in a big circle, but today I can't help myself. The walkers have disappeared from the tree-trunk, I climb over it and find the small stream. The water is high today, it gushes over the boulders, the water dark and slippery.

I really can't imagine why people want to travel the world when there is so much beauty at their fingertips.

December

It is late December, the last day of the year is approaching. The stubble sticks out above the snow on the old maize field but everything else is smooth and even, a woollen blanket covering the fields. The dog jumps from one side of the frozen stream to the other, back and forth, she is good at that. She's a traditional Frisian breed, ditch jumping is obviously in her blood.

I wipe the ice off the rungs of the hide with my mittens and climb up. The cold seeps through my trousers as I sit down, but the view is breathtaking. To my surprise, I see a bluethroat sitting on a branch of the old willow beside me, at eye level, its neck gleaming against the landscape. I've always dreamt of seeing a bluethroat but never have, let alone in winter. They are rare and always migrate away around September. They don't return until mid-March. Apparently this one forgot to migrate. I didn't know it was possible and wonder whether I'm imagining it.

'Why are you here?' I ask.

'For you.'

'Really?'

'Yes, of course.'

I think about this as the bluethroat flits around, drawing a small circle around me, its blue patch gleaming before my eyes. Then it perches on its branch again. It is the most beautiful thing I have ever seen, this slender bird with its cobalt neck. I'm not quite sure I believe he is here for me, but I decide to accept it gratefully.

It feels like he is entrusting himself to me and this makes me feel light.

'Why are you here?' the bluebird asks me.

I'm silent. I haven't known what I'm doing in this world for a long time, but the answer seems to be sitting beside me now.

'To see you,' I reply.

I hold out my hand, the bluebird flies up and lands on my finger. I feel its warm claws on my skin, its beating heart close to mine, soft feathers stroking my hand. He looks at me and I look back. Happiness floods through me, I can literally touch it.

The urge overwhelms me to put it into words or draw it, express it, share it with anyone who wants to hear it. It will live on, for sure. Perhaps the essence of happiness is a bird, the love of a bird.

'This will last forever,' I say.

'It will indeed,' says the bluethroat.

Encore

A little bird flies up from the potato field so fast I can't see what species it is.
'Looked like he was made of gold,' I say to W.

A little disappointed, I screen the potato beds, but he really has disappeared.

'I think it was a golden chit-chat,' he replies, straight-faced. 'Or a spud-catcher.'

I laugh.

It may seem in the previous stories that all this year I was walking alone, at most with the dog, but in reality W. was always with me. We stood together in the springtime as the swallows flew around us and together we skated on the singing ice. Together we watched the beaver emerge and disappear again into the stream.

It is drizzling, the path is muddy and I leap with difficulty over a large puddle. We stop at the meadow. There are three egrets at the edge of the mere, not close together but spaced a metre or two apart. They stare ahead, their wings hunched. They don't look very sociable to me, although they do remind me a little of myself. I never really need to be in a group with my peers.

W. takes my hand, my cold fingers find his warmth. I think about how long we have been walking together, here but everywhere else too. Although I don't like people around me, I always accept W. And while my conversations with birds take place some-where in between my head and the heavens, our conversations are always terrestrial, his words – and his silences – reaching a primal underlayer.

We walk on. Further along the sky is clearing, some blue appearing in the thick layers of grey. The egrets have taken off and are now flying low over us, their immense wings flapping slowly.

'Everything feels so big and so overwhelming sometimes,' I say.

I look up at the birds, they are a little awkward as they fly with their huge bodies, their legs dangling behind them. They're hardly gliding through the air.

W. nods.

In the wider world there is so much sorrow and grief, there is suffering and injustice, a constant impending doom. It is so close that sometimes we can do no more than cry silently.

We approach the road, the farmer is just arriving in his white van, he waves and we wave back. The trees and bushes here have formed an archway over the path. I'm always reminded of a cradle. The sun breaks through the clouds just as we go through it. The wind blows through the tall grass which changes colour in soft long strokes.

'We're lucky to have this,' I say.

Our fields, our meadows, the marsh, the poplars, the birds, ourselves. A little patch at the edge of everything, where the land folds around us, where everything changes as much as it stays the same.

'Here, everything is exactly as it should be,' I say.